HAPPY HALLOWEEN

TRICK OR TREAT

This book belongs to :

....

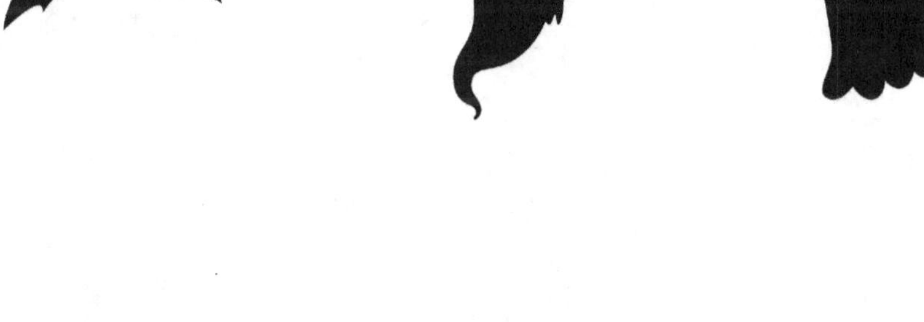

TRICK OR TREAT!
x

Boo

TRICK
OR
TREAT!

TRICK
OR
TREAT!
x

HALO
WEEN

TRICK OR TREAT!
x

TRICK OR TREAT!

TRICK
OR
TREAT!
x

TRICK OR TREAT!

TRICK
OR
TREAT!
x

TRICK
OR
TREAT!

TRICK
OR
TREAT!
x

TRICK
OR
TREAT!

TRICK OR TREAT!

TRICK
OR
TREAT!
x

TRICK
OR
TREAT!
x

TRICK
OR
TREAT!
x

TRICK OR TREAT!
x

R.I.P
1895 - 2

TRICK OR TREAT!

TRICK
OR
TREAT!
x

TRICK
OR
TREAT!

HAPPY
HALLOWEEN

TRICK
OR
TREAT!

TRICK
OR
TREAT!

TRICK OR TREAT!
x

I can't
be held
responsible
for stolen
candy

TRICK
OR
TREAT!
x

TRICK
OR
TREAT!
x

Ready
set
ghoul

TRICK OR TREAT!

Hocus Pocus I need coffee to focus

TRICK OR TREAT!

Halloween
and
chill

TRICK
OR
TREAT!
x

A real witch is nothing without her ghoul friends

TRICK
OR
TREAT!
x

Boo!

TRICK
OR
TREAT!

TRICK
OR
TREAT!
x

TRICK
OR
TREAT!
x

TRICK
OR
TREAT!
x

TRICK
OR
TREAT!

TRICK
OR
TREAT!

10¢ LB
15¢ LB
15¢ LB

TRICK OR TREAT!
x

TRICK OR TREAT!

Having a
bloody
good
time

TRICK OR TREAT!
x

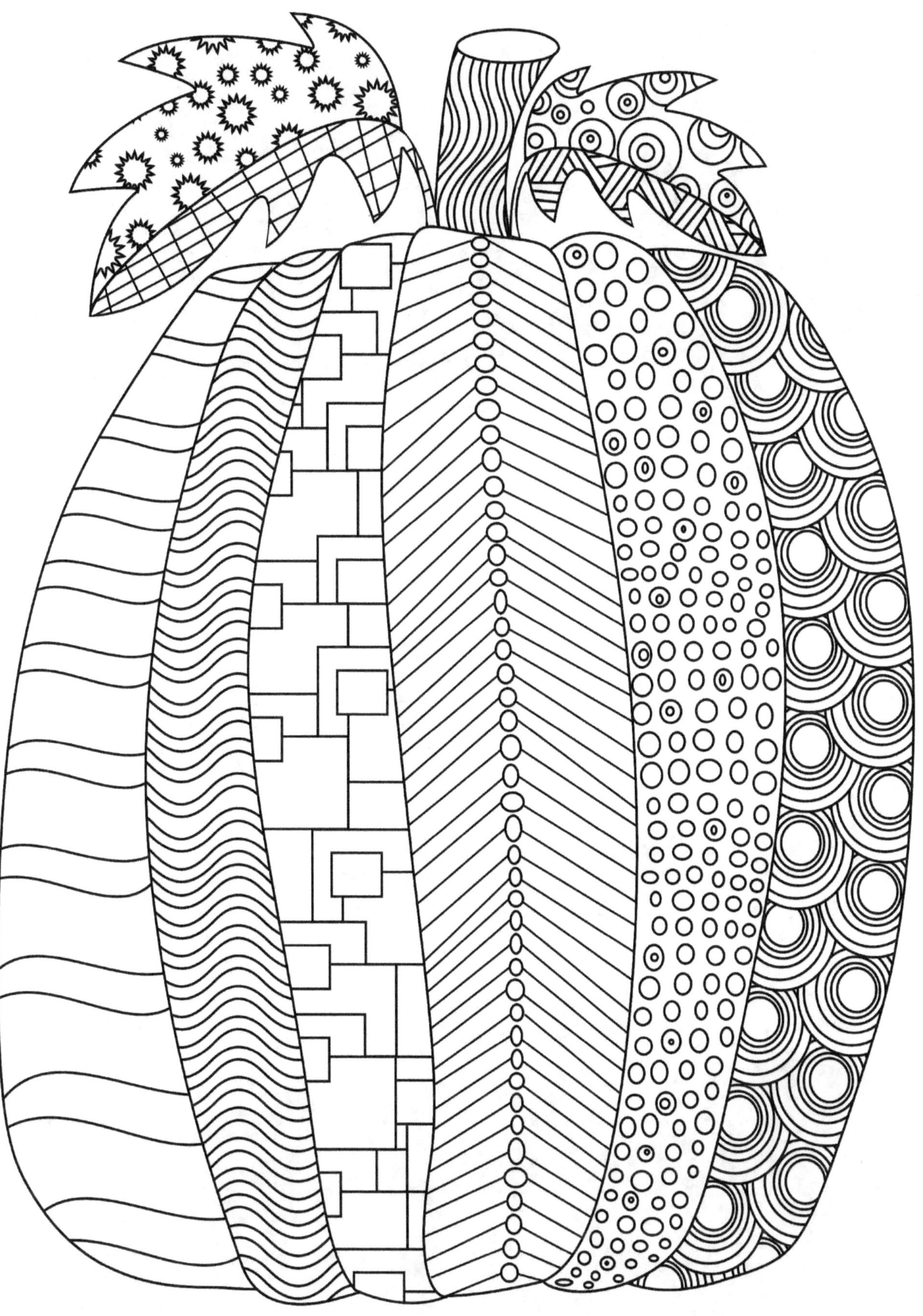

TRICK OR TREAT!

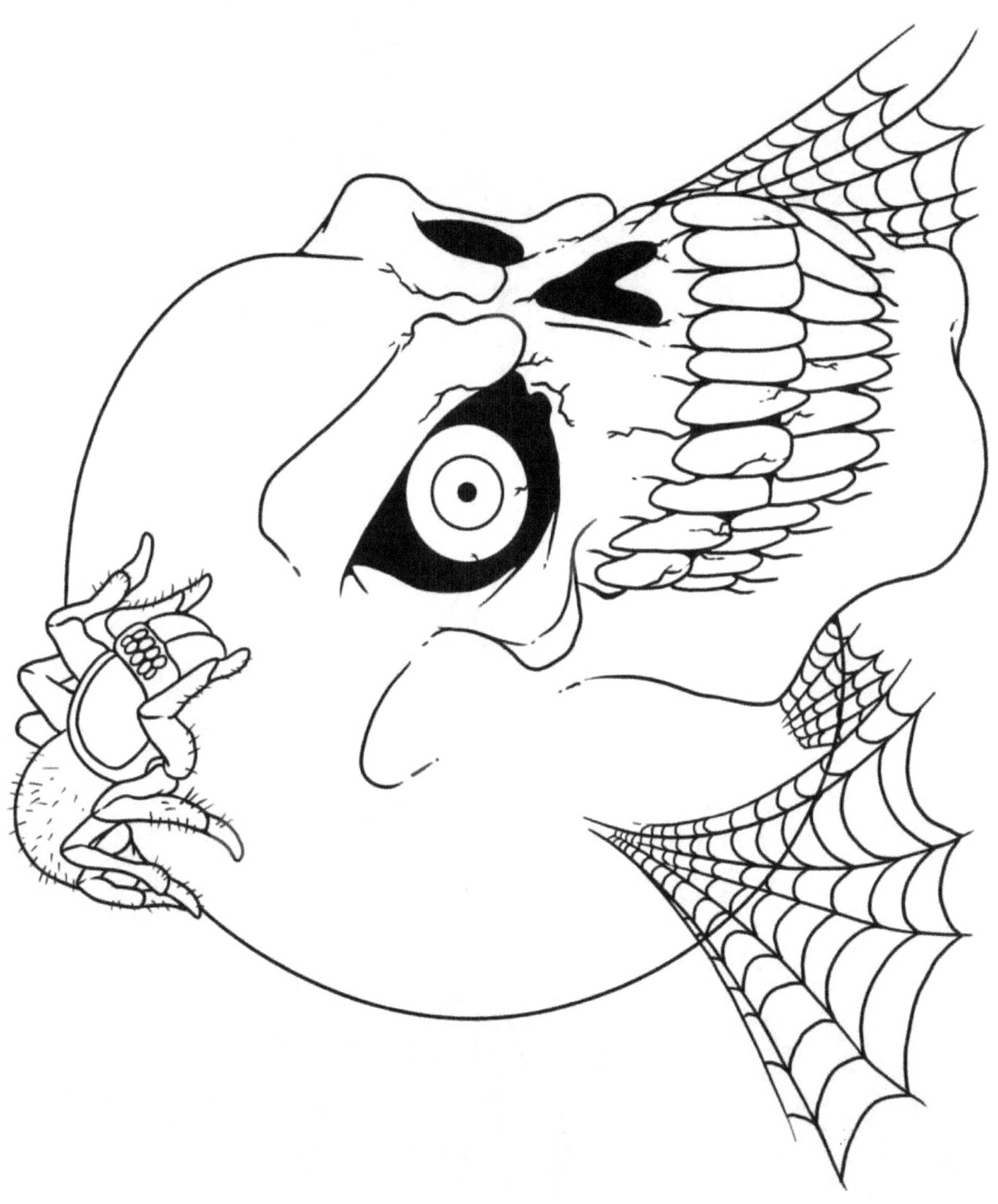

TRICK
OR
TREAT!
x

TRICK
OR
TREAT!

TRICK
OR
TREAT!
x

TRICK OR TREAT!

Boo
from
the
crew

TRICK OR TREAT!

I'd never ghost my ghouls

TRICK OR TREAT!
x

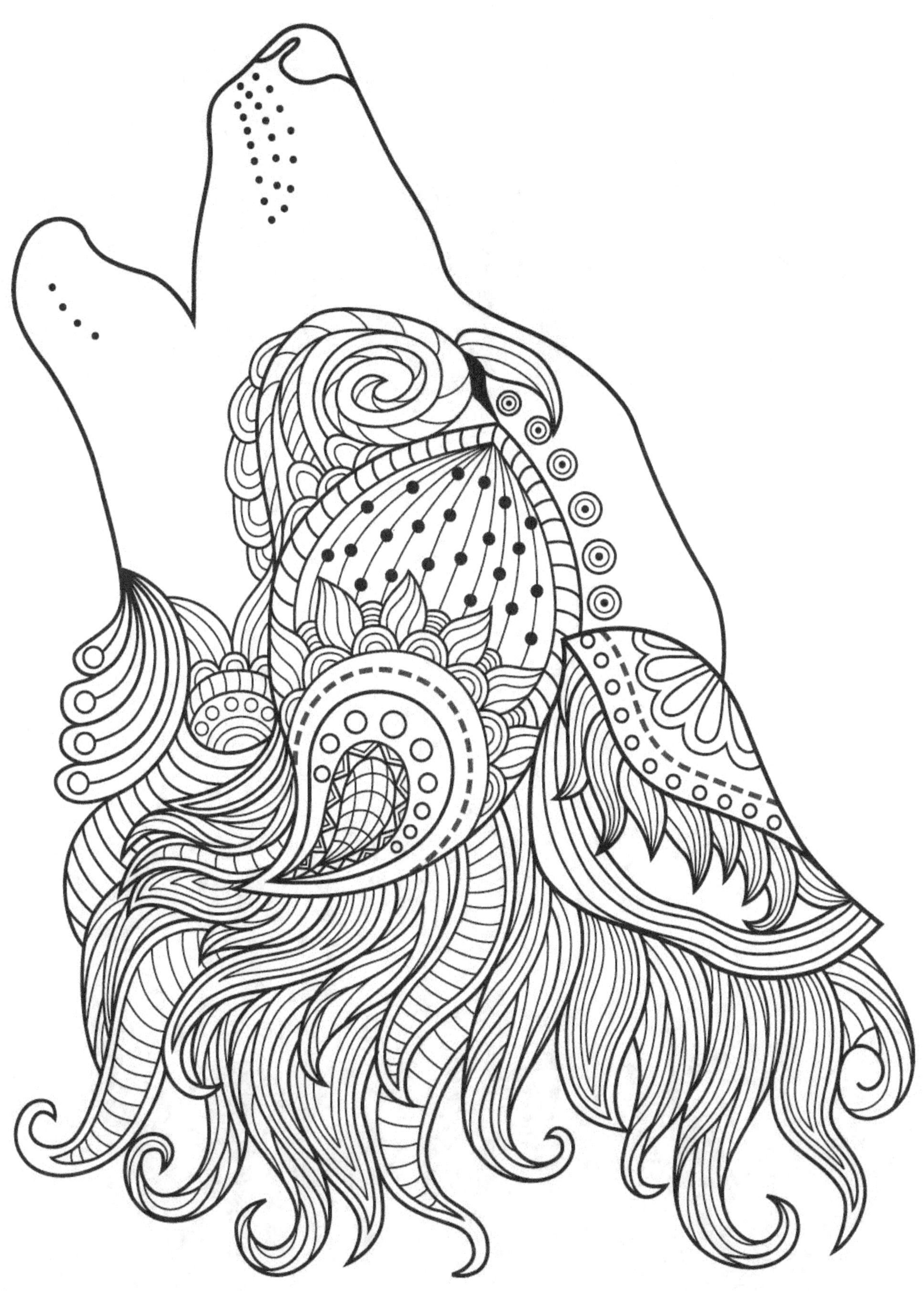

TRICK
OR
TREAT!
x

TRICK OR TREAT!
x

TRICK
OR
TREAT!

TRICK
OR
TREAT!
x

Dear Customer

A thousand thanks for purchasing this book. We really apreciate
We are a small family company and thanks to you, we exist.

We are young but we have big hearts and a big vision
We do our best to offer the HIGHEST QUALITY books for you to enjoy.
If you enjoy this book, we have a very modest request: please take a few seconds to leave us a review on this book's Amazon product page.

You can't imagine how pleased we are for the support, and we are doing our best to deliver you the best books. We wish you only the best, and if you want to reach us for inquiries please send an email at:

nikolas.norbert@yahoo.com

Sincerely

Nikolas Norbert